Discovery

The English-speaking World

英語世界

Janet Cameron

Series editor: Robert Hill
Editor: Chiara Gabutti
Design and art direction: Nadia Maestri
Computer graphics: Maura Santini
Picture research: Laura Lagomarsino, Alice Graziotin

書　　名：*The English-speaking World* 英語世界
作　　者：Janet Cameron
責任編輯：黃家麗　王朴真
封面設計：張毅
出　　版：商務印書館 (香港) 有限公司
　　　　　香港筲箕灣耀興道 3 號東滙廣場 8 樓
　　　　　http://www.commercialpress.com.hk
發　　行：香港聯合書刊物流有限公司
　　　　　香港新界大埔汀麗路 36 號中華商務印刷大廈 3 字樓
印　　刷：中華商務彩色印刷有限公司
　　　　　香港新界大埔汀麗路 36 號中華商務印刷大廈14 字樓
版　　次：2013 年 5 月第 1 版第 1 次印刷
　　　　　© 2013 商務印書館 (香港) 有限公司
　　　　　ISBN 978 962 07 1996 7
　　　　　Printed in Hong Kong

版權所有　不得翻印

Contents

The text is recorded in full.

 These symbols indicate the beginning and end of the passages linked to
the listening activities. 標誌表示與聽力練習有關的錄音片段開始和結束。

Before you read

1 What do you know?

Here are some places that will be mentioned in this book. How many do you know? See if you can match the pictures (A-E) to the names of the countries (1-5).

1 Canada   **2** New Zealand   **3** Kenya   **4** India   **5** Jamaica

2 Vocabulary

Most of these words are going to be important to the next chapter and all of them will appear in the book. Match each word in the box to its definition. Use the spaces and letters to help you.

colony   territory   settlement   settlers   govern   empire

0 A c o l o n y is a place which is controlled by another country. Usually there are a lot of people from the controlling country living there.

1 An _ m _ _ _ _ is a group of countries which are all controlled by one powerful person or government. It is like a kingdom, but much bigger.

2 A _ _ t _ _ _ _ _ _ is a colony in its first few years.
_ e _ _ _ _ _ _ are the people who live there.

3 To _ o _ _ _ _ means to control or rule.

4 A _ _ r _ _ _ _ _ _ is a land belonging to a country.

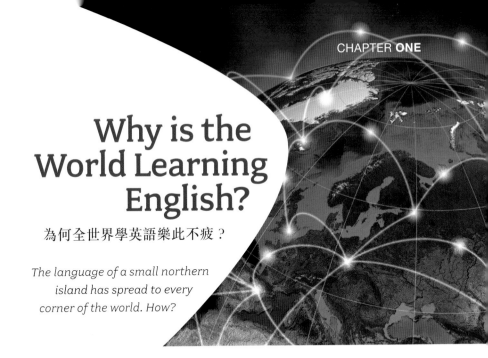

CHAPTER ONE

Why is the World Learning English?

為何全世界學英語樂此不疲？

The language of a small northern island has spread to every corner of the world. How?

English is one of the most widely spoken languages on earth. People in countries as far away from each other as Canada, Australia and Ireland speak English as their first, or native, language. Still more people have grown up speaking a different language, but are learning English for business or as a hobby. In fact, the British Council found that in the year 2000 there were over 750 million learners of English world-wide.

How did the use of English become so widespread [1] ? In modern times, Hollywood movies, television, and most recently the Internet have brought stories and characters from England and especially America into people's homes everywhere. But before this happened, English was already a global language. To find out why, we'll have to look back.

1. **widespread** : 廣泛

At first, English was only spoken in the country that we now know as England, and it was a very different language to the one that is used today. English began as a language spoken by the Angles, Saxons, and Jutes. These were Germanic tribes who came to England almost 2000 years ago. Over time this Anglo-Saxon language changed as it was mixed with the languages of other groups of people who invaded the island, such as the Danes, who brought words from Norse, and the Normans who brought French. Words from Latin and Greek were also added over time because these were considered the languages of higher knowledge. Gradually English changed and became the language we know today.

By the 15th century England was a strong country which was able to start exploring, setting up colonies, and expanding into other lands.

Exploration: North America and the Caribbean

In 1497 England sent explorers to 'the New World'. (Now we call this land North, South and Central America and the Caribbean.) At first England was only interested in trading, but later people came to set up colonies and live. But England was not the only country which was interested in the New World: England faced competition from Holland, Spain, France, and Portugal. In the 17th and 18th centuries there were wars between the European powers. Through these wars England gained control of most of North America, as well as Jamaica and Barbados.

But controlling people who lived a sixty-day journey away by sea was not always easy. From 1775-1783 the settlers of the colonies in America fought against Britain for their independence. Britain lost the American War of Independence, and lost the American colonies. After this, Britain concentrated on Asia, Africa and the Pacific.

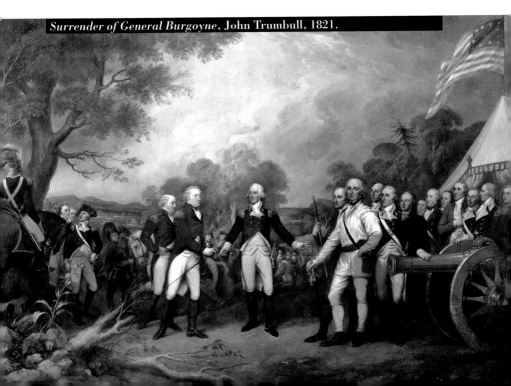

Surrender of General Burgoyne, John Trumbull, 1821.

The founding of Australia, Algernon Talmadge, 1788.

Australia, India and Africa

In 1770 Captain Cook, an English explorer, was the first European to land on the eastern coast of Australia. Australia was used by the British as a place to send prisoners from about 1788 to 1840, but later the colonies became strong and rich, especially after gold was found there.

In 1617 the British East India Company began to trade with India, and gradually it took control of parts of the country. After a rebellion in the mid-19ᵗʰ century, the British government took direct control, and most of India was ruled by Britain. India was Britain's most important colony for many years. It was called 'the jewel in the crown'.

In the 1800s Britain began adding African land to its empire. Other European countries competed for control of this continent. This was called 'the scramble [1] for Africa'. At the end of the 19ᵗʰ century England controlled the southern part of Africa and most of the east coast.

1.   **a scramble** : 爭奪

Countries and islands as far away as Hong Kong, Singapore, Fiji and Burma were also added to Britain's empire. In the 19th century, Britain was the greatest power in the world.

The Sun Never Sets

By 1922 the British Empire was at its highest point. Almost a quarter of the population of the world lived under English rule and the Empire covered one fourth of the earth's surface. It was said that "The sun never sets on the British Empire" because the countries which were controlled by Britain could be found all around the world. If it was night in England, for example, it might be day in India, or Antarctica.

9

The End of an Empire

This could not continue forever. Many countries wanted their independence. Also, it was expensive to govern so many different countries in so many parts of the world. Gradually Britain began giving independence to most of its colonies.

By the second half of the 20th century Britain had lost or given up most of its colonies. Today it still has 14 territories, including Bermuda and many small islands such as the Caymans in the Caribbean Sea and Fiji in the Pacific.

What was Left Behind: the Language

English is still spoken in many countries which were once part of the British Empire. In India, for example, English was the language of government for eighty-nine years, and so it is still widely spoken and is an additional official language. In countries like Canada and Australia, English was always a major language because of the English settlers who stayed and became the first citizens of new countries.

English continues to be an important language for countries all over the world. Let's look at some of them.

The text and **beyond**

1 Comprehension check

Look at the statements below. Decide if each statement is correct or incorrect. If it is correct, mark A. If it is not correct, mark B.

	A	B
1 English began to be spoken around the world about fifty years ago.	☐	☐
2 The New World was the name Europeans gave to North and South America and the Caribbean.	☐	☐
3 America became independent from England peacefully.	☐	☐
4 England sent prisoners to Australia until the 20th century.	☐	☐
5 In the 'scramble for Africa', European countries took African land.	☐	☐
6 England once controlled almost 25% of the world's people and land.	☐	☐
7 Today England doesn't control any other countries.	☐	☐

2 Talk about it

Talk about these questions with a friend, and share your answers with the rest of the class.

1 Is it right for one country to control another country? What are some problems that could happen?

2 Does your own country control any other lands? Did your own country ever have colonies?

3 Why is it strange to say that people 'discovered' land in North America or Australia? Who was living there at the time?

Read the text below and choose the correct word for each space. For each question, mark the letter next to the correct word — A, B, C or D.

A Famous English Queen

Queen Victoria ruled England at a time when the British Empire was very strong. She is a symbol of England and of a time in history. Victoria became queen when she was only 18 years (**0**) ....**B**..... . When she (**1**) .... twenty-one she married her cousin Albert. The two were very happy together and had nine children and 42 grandchildren. When Albert died (**2**) .... 1861, Victoria was (**3**) .... sad that she did not appear in public (**4**) .... ten years, and she wore black dresses for the rest of her life.

Victoria never married (**5**) .... , but for years she was very close to one of her servants, who was a man from Scotland named James Brown. Their story is told in the film *Mrs. Brown* (1997). Another film, *The Young Victoria* (2009), is (**6**) .... her first years as queen and her marriage to Albert.

She became very popular in England as the empire became (**7**) .... successful. Victoria was queen for 63 years, (**8**) .... 1837 to 1901, which is longer (**9**) .... any other English queen or king. This time in history is known (**10**) .... 'the Victorian era'.

0	**A** aged	**B** old	**C** older	**D** young
1	**A** is	**B** had	**C** was	**D** until
2	**A** in	**B** on	**C** then	**D** at
3	**A** such	**B** very	**C** so	**D** felt
4	**A** during	**B** while	**C** at	**D** for
5	**A** more	**B** again	**C** not	**D** any
6	**A** about	**B** around	**C** for	**D** told
7	**A** more	**B** most	**C** better	**D** well
8	**A** for	**B** ago	**C** from	**D** yet
9	**A** then	**B** as	**C** so	**D** than
10	**A** as	**B** by	**C** like	**D** from

4 Plan your journey (part 1)
Look through the chapter again. What countries have been written about? Would you like to visit any of these places? Imagine that you are planning a journey around the world, and can go to any of the places here. Which places would you visit? Why? How long would you spend in each place? Write your top three choices.
Look back on this question as you read through the book. Maybe you will change your mind!

Hollywood and the Internet have brought stories and characters from America into people's homes.

We use the present perfect to talk about 1) events that happened at an unspecified time in the past, 2) events or states that began in the past and have continued until now, 3) recent actions with effects in the present. However, we use the simple past to talk about events or states that are finished and happened at a specific time in the past.

5 Past perfect and simple past 過去完成時和一般過去時
Complete the sentences by using the present perfect or the simple past. Choose the best verb from the box:

die   travel   love   live   land

0 Thousands of people ....*have died*.... from smoking-related illnesses.
Over a thousand people ....*died*......... from smoking-related illnesses in 2007.

1 I .... you for years, and I still do!
I .... you, but now I never want to see you again.

2 Jerry .... in that little house until he died.
Sandra .... here for six months, but next year she might move.

3 In 1770 Captain Cook .... on the shores of Australia.
Many European explorers .... on these shores over the years.

4 .... you ever .... to Africa?
Yes, I .... there in 2005.

Before you read

1 **What do you know?**

What do you already know about Australia and New Zealand? Look at the pictures with a friend and talk about them. Do you know these places, people and animals? How are they connected with Australia and New Zealand?

2 **Vocabulary**

Match the sentence beginnings (1-5) and endings (A-E) to form sentences. The <u>underlined</u> words in each sentence will be important in the next chapter.

1 The beliefs, ideas, art, and knowledge of a group of people ...
2 Irish people came to live in America in the 1800's. They had children, ...
3 A <u>plateau</u> is an area which is high ...
4 There are many different <u>species</u> of trees, ...
5 People from England, America, and Australia all speak English, ...

A their children had children, and their <u>descendants</u> are still living there.
B such as palm trees to evergreens.
C but they have different <u>accents</u>, or ways or pronouncing their words.
D is also called their <u>culture</u>.
E but flat, like a mountain with no peak.

CHAPTER TWO

Australia and New Zealand

澳洲、新西蘭英語

Life 'down under': beaches, bright lights and stunning natural beauty.

Australia

Australia is one of the largest countries on earth — it is the sixth largest country after Russia, Canada, China, the USA and Brazil — and it is the biggest island. Most of Australia, especially the centre, is covered by a desert called the Outback. Australia also has mountains, rainforests, beautiful beaches, and modern cities.

The Story

Hundreds of years ago Britain sent prisoners to this land, but some parts of Australia were for free settlers. This does not mean that the people who first came to Australia were dangerous criminals. At this time in history there was terrible poverty in England, and you could be sent to prison for stealing bread, or even executed for cutting down a tree.

The journey to Australia from England was long and difficult. Prisoners often spent over six months on a boat from England to Australia. Many of the people on the first 'prison ship' to Australia died because they were not given enough food to survive during their first few months in this new country.

But over the years prisoners were given their freedom, more people arrived because gold was found, and Australia became a rich modern country. Now it is one of the best places to live in the world.

Prison ship ready to sail from England to Australia.

The Language

English is the first language of Australia. But the accent and some of the words are very different from English in England or America. Most people know that in Australia you say 'G'Day!' to say hello, but you might not know that 'fair dinkum' means 'true, or real', 'arvo' is the afternoon, 'take a squizz' means 'to look' and a 'chook' is a chicken. It is very difficult to say why these words began to be used. Some people think 'squizz' comes from a mix of 'squint' and 'quiz', and 'chook' may come from an old word for 'dear', or from the clucking noise that chickens make. There is a story that 'dinkum' comes from the Chinese 'ding gum', or 'real gold', but this is probably not true.

Many of the people in Australia are descendants of the English or Irish people who came to the country in the 18th and 19th centuries. But there are some native people, called Aborigines, who have lived in Australia for thousands of years. At one time there were over 300 languages spoken by the Aboriginal people but only 70 of them are still used.

People from many other countries are still coming to Australia to live and they are bringing their own languages with them. The second most common language that people speak at home is Italian. The third and fourth are Greek and Chinese.

Australian Aborigins.

Sydney Opera House.

Australia: Places

Sydney is the biggest city in Australia and is an important centre for business, culture and sports. It is the home of the famous Sydney Opera House, which is a symbol of Australia and one of the most well-known buildings in the world. Bondi Beach, another well-known place, is 7 kilometres outside of Sydney, and you can often see people surfing on the waves or playing beach volleyball there.

The Outback is also well-known and a symbol of Australia. Ayers Rock is here. It is a plateau which is 348 metres high and 9 kilometres around. It is made of sandstone which changes colour with the light and can seem light-brown, or deep red. People call it 'the Heart of Australia'. It is also very important to the myths and legends of the Aborigines.

Temperatures in the Outback can be high, in fact the hottest months have average temperatures of over 35 degrees Celsius. One small town, called Coober Pedy, was built with most of its houses and shops underground. There is a golf course, but it is too hot during the day to play there. Instead people play golf at night with golf balls that glow in the dark.

Ayers Rock.

Animals of Australia

Because it is an island, many of
Australia's animals, birds, plants
and trees are special to this country.
You will not find them living naturally
anywhere else. There are kangaroos, of
course, and there are also large birds called
emus, which are like ostriches but smaller. People have
told stories about emus that approach humans in the wild. They
sometimes poke[1] people and then run away, as if they are playing a
game. Kookaburras are another kind of Australian bird. They have
a strange cry that sounds like a human laugh. Koalas are a symbol
of Australia. They are commonly called 'bears', but this is not true.
Perhaps the strangest Australian animal is the platypus. This
animal has fur and is warm-blooded, like a mammal, but lays eggs
and has feet and a bill like a duck's.

In the past Europeans brought their own animals with them,
or animals have been introduced to Australia to control pests[2].
The results have been terrible. Rabbits
and cats have destroyed several species
of plants, and cane toads, which are
poisonous and increasing
in numbers every day,
are causing problems for
animals, plants and people.

1. **poke** : 撞
2. **pests** : 害蟲

Food and Hobbies in Australia

You can find a lot of different kinds of food in Australia. Vegemite is a dark brown paste which is produced from yeast extract. People spread it on toast. It has a bitter salty taste and many people  who aren't from Australia don't like it. But there are a lot of other kinds of food which are more popular with visitors. Seafood is part of Australian cooking. People also enjoy Asian food.

You can eat meat from kangaroos, although this is not something Australians would eat every day — a recent survey found that only 14.5% of Australians ate kangaroo meat more than four times a year. Crocodile and emu meat are also available, but aren't widely popular. Cooking food on a barbecue, or 'barbie' as Australians call it, is common. A barbecue on the beach is a great way to relax, and Australians do this often.

Other activities are surfing, scuba diving, fishing, and playing sports. The most popular sports are cricket, rugby, and a special kind of football called 'Australian Rules'. This game is a mix of soccer and rugby, and can be very tough.

Australian Stars and Backpackers

Many Australians have become famous in other countries. There are pop stars like Kylie Minogue, bands such as the old favourite AC/DC and actors like Mel Gibson, Nicole Kidman, Hugh Jackman and Heath Ledger. You might remember movies which were set in Australia, like the *Mad Max* series from the 1980s, *Babe* (1995), or *Strictly Ballroom* (1993).

Mel Gibson.

Young Australians have a tradition of travelling. A flight from Australia to the nearest European city takes a long time — sometimes over 24 hours. Because of this, young people who have finished university or high school often decide to go travelling and see the world before they settle down [1]. They try to visit as many countries as possible. It is common to meet young Australians who travel for a year or more around Europe, North America, and the rest of the world, carrying nothing but a backpack.

Times have changed since Australia was a British colony. These days many Australians see themselves as part of Asia rather than Europe, and in secondary schools Japanese and Chinese might be offered for study instead of European languages such as French. Immigration from Africa, India, and China as well as Europe, is also changing the country. Australia's future is unknown, but it will probably be bright.

1. **settle down**：穩定

21

A scene from *The Lord of the Rings*.

New Zealand: Land and Animals

About 1,500 kilometres east of Australia you will find New Zealand. New Zealand is one of the last places on earth where humans came to live, when the Maori people arrived there roughly 3000 years ago. It is a land full of differences. You can find high snowy mountains, green farmlands, sandy beaches and even volcanoes. The movies of *The Lord of the Rings* series were filmed here. It is easy to see why: you can find a whole world of beautiful scenery in these two islands.

New Zealand is a quieter place than Australia. Many people say that New Zealanders are more friendly and relaxed. There are fewer than 4.5 million people living in an area of 268,000 square kilometres. Farming is a major part of the economy here, especially sheep farming. Growing grapes and making wine is also important.

There are many animals that can only be found on these islands, especially birds. Unfortunately, when humans came to New Zealand they hunted and brought rats and cats with them, and so many kinds of birds died out. The most famous New Zealand bird is the kiwi. Kiwis are about the size of chickens, with long legs and beaks, and they can't fly. Kiwis have become a symbol of New Zealand. In fact, it is common to call a person from New Zealand a 'kiwi'.

People and Places of New Zealand

But New Zealand is not only a wild place. Auckland, on the North Island, is the biggest city in New Zealand and is a modern city of many cultures. Wellington is a small city which is well known for its art and night life. Christchurch, on the South Island, is often called 'The Garden City' because of its parks. Unfortunately, Christchurch was badly damaged by earthquakes in 2010 and 2011.

Roughly 98% of the people in New Zealand speak English. The second official language is Maori, which is spoken by the native Maori people.

The Maori have traditions and culture that are hundreds of years old. Their art, especially tattoos, uses detailed, complex patterns and strong colours. When the New Zealand rugby team (they are called the All Blacks because of their team colours) play, they do a special war dance before each game called the *kappa haka*. This is an old Maori dance. They do this to frighten the other team. The All Blacks are very successful, so this must work! Other sports which are played in New Zealand are cricket and netball [1].

1. **netball**：無板籃球

The All Blacks performing their war dance before the game.

Famous New Zealanders include the writer Katherine Mansfield, the actor Russel Crowe, the comedy music group Flight of the Conchords and the film director Sir Peter Jackson, who directed *The Lord of the Rings* trilogy.

Remember: don't confuse New Zealanders with Australians. The two countries may seem similar, but not to the people who live there!

Portrait of Katherine Mansfield,
Anne E. Rice, 1918.

Russel Crowe.

The text and **beyond**

PET 1 **Comprehension –practice**

For each question, mark the letters next to the correct answer — A, B, C or D.

1 Most of the first people from Europe who came to Australia were

   A ☐ rich people who had broken the law in England.

   B ☐ dangerous criminals from England.

   C ☐ poor people who had broken the law.

   D ☐ people who were looking for gold around Melbourne.

2 What happened when new animals were brought to Australia?

   A ☐ They formed new species of animals.

   B ☐ They upset the balance of nature.

   C ☐ They destroyed many species of cane toads.

   D ☐ They helped to control insects or pests.

3 Why do young people from Australia travel for long periods of time?

   A ☐ It takes a long time to leave Australia.

   B ☐ They see themselves as part of Europe.

   C ☐ They don't have enough money to travel more than once.

   D ☐ Australia is not a good place to live.

4 How is New Zealand different from Australia?

   A ☐ There is beautiful scenery.

   B ☐ Farming is part of the economy.

   C ☐ It is quieter and some say it is more friendly.

   D ☐ The Aborigines live there.

5 The Maori people

   A ☐ came to New Zealand after the Europeans.

   B ☐ live mainly in Wellington.

   C ☐ are frightened of playing rugby.

   D ☐ have their own language and culture.

PET ❷ Practice – reading

The people below are thinking about taking a holiday in Australia. Decide which holiday package tour would be the most suitable for the following people. Mark the correct letter (A-E) next to the right person (1-3).

1 ☐ Bella is on holiday with her two small children. She is looking for something fun to do with them. Her son loves being outside and her daughter likes cute animals.

2 ☐ Paul is retired. He wants to relax, make friends, and meet beautiful women. He doesn't drink but he loves to cook, chat and have fun.

3 ☐ Colleen is from the countryside and she wants a city break. She loves reading and art, and is looking for experiences that will make her think about life.

Tours

A Historical Australia — Experience the most important historical places in Australia. We'll go far away from the usual city museums to the old prison colony in Tasmania and the small country town where Ned Kelly lived.

B Wild Australia — Join our lively bus as we go on an exciting journey through wildlife parks and say hello to some of Australia's famous native animals. You can't feed the koalas, but they won't mind if you take a picture! Have fun!

C Bondi Beach Party — We're getting the barbecue ready for you! Australians and other travellers are waiting to start the biggest party of the year! If you like beach volleyball, swimming, or just meeting friendly people, this is your holiday!

D A Cultural Tour of Sydney and Melbourne — Our tour covers the best museums, art galleries and theatres of these cultural centres. We conclude with an evening of works by Mozart performed at the Sydney Opera House. Book it today!

E City Night Life — Dance until you drop! Join our group of twenty young people from Australia and all over the world as we spend the nights in the clubs and bars of Sydney! You can spend the days recovering! Be prepared to party!

TRINITY PRACTICE – GRADE 4

3 Speaking - Sport and Hobbies

In Australia people like to have a barbecue, go surfing or scuba diving, or play sports.

- What do you like to do in your free time?
- Do you have a special hobby, or is there a sport you like to play?
- How often do you do it?
- When was the last time you did it?

Prepare a short talk about your favourite sports or hobbies. In your talk, be sure that you answer these questions. Practice with a friend.

4 Plan your journey (part 2)

Now imagine that you have two weeks to spend in Australia and New Zealand. What places would you like to visit?

List your top three choices. Next, ask your friend about his or her top three choices and write them below. Ask your friend why he or she has chosen these places.

Your top three
1 ....
2 ....
3 ....
Your friend's top three
1 ....
2 ....
3 ....

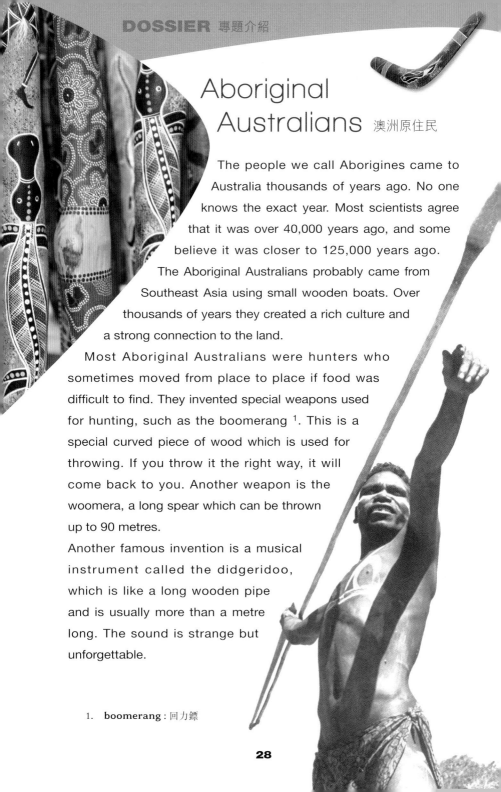

Aboriginal Australians 澳洲原住民

The people we call Aborigines came to Australia thousands of years ago. No one knows the exact year. Most scientists agree that it was over 40,000 years ago, and some believe it was closer to 125,000 years ago. The Aboriginal Australians probably came from Southeast Asia using small wooden boats. Over thousands of years they created a rich culture and a strong connection to the land.

Most Aboriginal Australians were hunters who sometimes moved from place to place if food was difficult to find. They invented special weapons used for hunting, such as the boomerang [1]. This is a special curved piece of wood which is used for throwing. If you throw it the right way, it will come back to you. Another weapon is the woomera, a long spear which can be thrown up to 90 metres.

Another famous invention is a musical instrument called the didgeridoo, which is like a long wooden pipe and is usually more than a metre long. The sound is strange but unforgettable.

---

1. **boomerang** : 回力鏢

Aboriginal Australian culture and beliefs are interesting and unique. One of the most important ideas to the culture is the Dreamtime or Dreaming. It is difficult to say exactly what the Dreamtime is. One explanation is that it is the time before the world began. In this time, different spirits made the land that we live in now. Some of these spirits were people, some were animals, and some were plants. But people also believe that the Dreamtime is not exactly part of the past, that it is still with us today. We exist in the Dreamtime before we are born and go back to it after we die. You can also say that a person's ideas and beliefs are their own 'Dreaming'.

Uluru, which is now the name in Australia for Ayers Rock, has a strong connection with Dreamtime and the spirits who made the land. It is still used by Aboriginals as an important cultural place. Legends say that in the Dreamtime before the world was made, two tribes of sprits were going to meet for a feast. One tribe didn't meet the other tribe (they were stopped by beautiful 'lizard women') and so there was a great battle. That day, as the story says, evil was put on earth in the form of the dingo (a wild dog). After the battle, both the tribe leaders were killed. The earth rose up in sadness because of the fighting and became Uluru.

There are other Aboriginal legends and strange characters. The most famous is the bunyip. This is a large monster that lives in rivers and swamps [1]. It has a dog-like face, a horse's tail and large teeth, and it eats travellers.

Aboriginal art is important to its culture. In the past, people painted with colours made from natural minerals and clay. They painted on rocks and in caves, and you can still see these paintings today. Ubirr in North Australia is a good place to go to see the cave paintings. Paintings were also made on tree bark [2]. This is still continued today, with modern paint and equipment.

When Europeans arrived in Australia in the 18th century, there were problems. At the time of Captain Cook's arrival, there were over 250 tribes or nations of Aboriginal Australians – some say the number was close to 500 – and most of these tribes had their own languages. Europeans took the land which belonged to Aborigines, and they also brought diseases. At the beginning of the 20th century, the population of Aboriginal Australians was about two-thirds lower than their population before the arrival of Europeans.

---

1. **swamps** : 沼澤
2. **tree bark** : 樹皮

A scene from *The Rabbit Proof Fence*.

Aborigines had to live with racism and unfair treatment for many years as well. In some areas they were not allowed to vote in elections. From 1869 until the 1960s Aboriginal children were often taken away from their families because people thought they would have better lives with whites. People who were taken from their parents in this way were called 'the stolen generation'. The film *Rabbit Proof Fence* (2002) tells this story. Poverty, unemployment and racism also continued to be problems for Aboriginal Australians. The government would also not agree that the land in Australia belonged to Aborigines and was taken from them.

In the 1960's there were protests, and slowly people became aware of the problems of Aboriginal Australians. Now most people in Australia understand that these people were treated very badly and the government is slowly trying to make their lives better. In 1985, Uluru was given back to the Aboriginal people. Aborigines have become successful and famous in Australia, as actors, writers, musicians, athletes and more. In 2000 Cathy Freeman, an Aboriginal Australian and a great short-distance runner, lit the flame in the Olympic Games in Sydney.

1 Comprehension check
Answer the questions.

1 Where did the Aboriginal Australians come from?
2 How long have they been in Australia?
3 What is Dreamtime?
4 What is a *bunyip*?
5 What happened after Europeans arrived?
6 What were some problems for Aboriginal people in the 20th century?
7 What is one good thing that the government has done for Aboriginal people?

Before you read

1 Southern Africa: What do you already know?
Do you recognise these people, places and things? Match the pictures
(A-F) to the words (1-6). What do you think is the connection between
these pictures and southern Africa? Check again after you read Chapter 3.

1 leopard
2 the Kalahari desert
3 diamonds
4 Victoria Falls
5 Nelson Mandela
6 World Cup

2 Strange new words!
Read the questions and try to guess the answers. Choose A, B or C.
Then, read Chapter 3 and check — were you right?

1 The Boers were people from

A ☐ England, Scotland
   and Wales

B ☐ Holland, Germany,
   Belgium and France

C ☐ northern and
   western Africa

2 In South African slang,
   'dankie' means

A ☐ Thank you
B ☐ Go away
C ☐ Congratulations

3 A vuvuzela is

A ☐ A musical
   instrument

B ☐ An animal with
   long horns

C ☐ A kind of ice-cream

3 A baobab is

A ☐ A kind of monkey
B ☐ A type of song
C ☐ A kind of tree

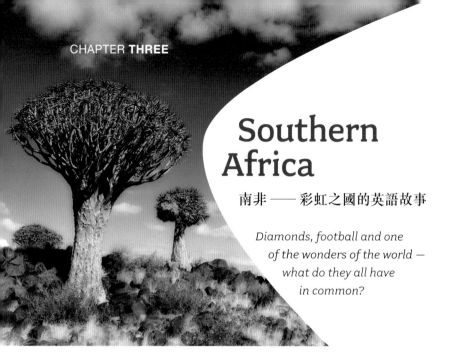

CHAPTER THREE

Southern Africa

南非 —— 彩虹之國的英語故事

*Diamonds, football and one
of the wonders of the world —
what do they all have
in common?*

The southern tip of Africa is known as southern Africa. It has
many countries which use English as an official language. This
part of Africa has deserts, forests, grasslands ¹, mountains and
beaches. But its most valuable possession is beneath the ground.

Southern Africa is rich with diamonds, gold, platinum and
other valuable minerals. Mining is an important part of southern
Africa's economy.

Southern Africa: the Story

In the late 19ᵗʰ century European countries, including Britain,
fought to control this part of Africa and its diamonds and gold.
These countries took land from native Africans and set up
colonies. Many of these colonies were passed from one European
country to another, especially after World War I when Germany

1.   **grasslands** : 草原

lost its African colonies.

Britain controlled many countries in southern Africa. Most of these countries did not become independent until the 1960s or later. They were once a great source of money for Britain, especially after a railway was built. This railway connected the Suez Canal in the north of Africa with the diamonds and gold of southern Africa.

Today all the countries of southern African are independent. But there are some problems. In some places the people are very poor. When rain doesn't fall, there is often not enough food for everyone. There have been problems with wars, and governments taking too much power. Diseases such as AIDS are a serious problem for southern Africa.

Animals

The land is unique and people come from all over the world to see it. You can find many famous animals in southern Africa. There are white rhinoceroses [1], which are the largest land animals except elephants.

1. **rhinoceroses** : 犀牛

Wildebeests are animals that are like buffalo or wild cows. They sometimes travel together in groups of over 500, and when they are running they can reach speeds of 80 kilometres per hour. There are also lions, leopards, and impalas (a kind of antelope). Vervet monkeys, which have dark faces and light grey fur, can be found in southern Africa, and elephants are common.

There are problems when humans and large animals such as elephants, rhinoceroses and wildebeests share the same land. Farmers' crops have been destroyed. Should they be allowed to kill these large animals? Some animals are becoming rare and may die out [1]. On the other hand, farmers also need to make a living. There is no easy answer.

Food and Culture

There are many special kinds of food in southern Africa. A porridge made of ground corn [2] is common. This dish is served with meat gravy and is called *pap*. Meat is very important to southern African cooking. *Bobotie* is mincemeat which is baked with an egg topping. *Boerewors* is a kind of spicy sausage cooked on a barbecue. The country of South Africa produces wine which is very good and is sold internationally.

1. **die out** : 滅絕
2. **ground corn** : 磨碎的粟米

The people of southern Africa love sports. Rugby and cricket are popular, and so is soccer. Music and dancing are also an important part of life here. In the 1980s the music of the country of South Africa became internationally famous when the American singer Paul Simon recorded an album (*Graceland*, 1986) with a South African musical group called Ladysmith Black Mombazo. The success of this album led to international attention for more southern African artists.

Let's look at some of the countries of Southern Africa.

South Africa: The Story

South Africa was established in 1909 and was a British colony. Before this, native Africans lived here. There were also people from Holland, Germany, Belgium and France — mainly Protestant farmers who settled in South Africa in the 17th century when the Dutch were trading in the area. They were called the Boers.

The British began to be interested in this part of the world in the 19th century, especially after diamonds were found in 1867 and gold in 1884. Wars were fought between the British, the Boers and the native Africans over this land, and the British won.

Boers ready to fight during the Boer War, 1900 ca.

In 1931 South Africa became independent. There were three races in South Africa: Afrikaners, who were the descendants of the Boers, British people, and native Africans. The native Africans had the highest population and were the poorest. The system of Apartheid began in 1948 and continued until about 1990. Under this system white citizens lived separately from non-white citizens

Nelson Mandela.

and whites had all the power. Nelson Mandela protested against Apartheid, and was put in prison by the government for 27 years. In 1990 Nelson Mandela was released and four years later he became the first Black president of South Africa.

The Language

English is spoken in South Africa, along with a language called Afrikaans, which is the language of the Afrikaners and is very close to Dutch. South Africa has nine other official languages; all of them are native African languages.

The English accent is special to this country and there are many odd slang words. South Africans who speak English might say 'dankie' for 'thank you' or 'howzit' for 'hello'.

Penguins at Boulders Beach.

Places

Kruger National Park is over 20,000 square kilometres and has many wild animals and unique trees, including huge baobabs. Until it split in half in 2009, the largest baobab tree in the world, the Glencoe Baobab, was in Kruger Park. The trunk was 47 metres around and 16 metres across. (Now the largest Baobab is the Sunland Baobab, also in South Africa.)

If you visit South Africa you could also ride an ostrich in the town of Oudtshoorn in the west or swim with penguins at Boulders Beach near Cape Town.

The World Cup

In 2010 the FIFA World Cup, the world's biggest soccer competition, was held in South Africa — the first time any African country had hosted the games. The 2010 World Cup was also known for the sound of vuvuzelas — long noisy horns. Some people who watched the games at home thought that their TV sets were broken because of the noise!

Reed dance in Swaziland.

Swaziland and Lesotho

Within South Africa there are two small countries which have their own traditions and laws. Both of these countries have English as an official language, and both were once colonies of Britain. Lesotho became independent from Britain in 1966 and Swaziland in 1968.

Swaziland is bordered by South Africa on three sides. It is a country of only 17,000 square kilometres, but you can find mountains, plains and rain forests here. Swaziland is also known for the tradition of the Reed Dance in August and September, when young girls cut reeds, present them to the King's mother, and dance.

Lesotho is another small country inside South Africa. It is sometimes called the Mountain Kingdom because it is located in the mountains; in fact, it is the only independent country which is all mountains. More than 75% of the land is at least 1,800 metres high.

Both of these small countries have had problems recently. Many of the people are very poor. AIDS is also a terrible problem. Half of all people aged 20-30 in Swaziland have this disease, and almost a third of the population of Lesotho.

Namibia

English is also an official language in Namibia. Namibia was a German colony from 1884 to 1915, when it was taken over by South Africa, and it did not gain independence from South Africa until 1990. The country covers over 800,000 square kilometres but has a population of about 2 million people, which is only 2.5 people for every square kilometre. Namibia is mostly desert; in fact, the sun shines here for about 300 days a year. Mining is very important to Namibia — the desert area along the coast is one of the richest places for diamonds on earth.

Zambia and Zimbabwe

These two countries were once called Northern and Southern Rhodesia, after Cecil Rhodes, who claimed the land for Britain in 1894. Today both countries still use English as an official language. Both of these countries are on high plateaus of 900-1500 metres. Zambia and Zimbabwe share the beautiful Victoria Falls, the largest waterfall in the world. The falls are 1.6 kilometres wide and 800 metres high. In the Kololo language, they are called "Mosi-oa-Tunya", which means 'the thundering smoke'.

Victoria Falls.

Zambia is north of Zimbabwe. Most of the people there live in cities, especially the capital, Lusaka. Football is important to Zambians, and their team is very good. In 1996 they were 15th in the world, the highest ever for a team from southern Africa. People in Zambia all agree that the best team the country ever had was the 1993 team. Sadly, the team were all killed in a plane crash that year.

Zimbabwe only became independent in 1980. It has many of the same problems as Zambia and other Southern African countries, especially with food shortages. The actions of its government, such as attacking its own citizens, controlling the media and the courts, and killing political opponents, have made other countries refuse to trade with Zimbabwe in the past, and this has made its problems worse.

Botswana

Botswana has a growing economy and a strong culture. There are many parks to protect the animals that live there. There is Chobe National Park, which has the most elephants per square kilometre in the world, and there are also special parks for

rhinoceroses and another one for flamingos [1]. This is one of the only places in the world where you can still see large packs of African wild dogs.

The Kalahari Desert covers 70% of the land here, and people are worried that the desert is growing. No one knows what this will to do the people or the animals of Botswana.

1.　**flamingos**：紅鶴

The text and **beyond**

1 Comprehension

Match the statements (1-12) with the countries they are about (A-G).
You may use each country more than once.

A South Africa   **B** Swaziland   **C** Lesotho   **D** Namibia
E Zambia   **F** Zimbabwe   **G** Botswana

1   ☐   Afrikaans is spoken here.
2   ☐   This country is entirely in the mountains.
3   ☐ ☐   Victoria Falls is here.
4   ☐   The country is very large and the population is small.
5   ☐   This country is extremely rich in diamonds.
6   ☐   White citizens had more power than black citizens here for
       many years.
7   ☐   Tourists can ride ostriches and swim with penguins here.
8   ☐   Half of all people in their twenties here have a serious disease.
9   ☐ ☐   These countries were once named after an Englishman.
10 ☐   The sun shines for most of the year here.
11 ☐   This country is mostly covered by the Kalahari Desert.
12 ☐   Is probably the best southern African country at football.

TRINITY PRACTICE – GRADE 5

2 Speaking – Music

Prepare a short talk. Be sure that you answer these questions.
Practice with a friend.

•   What kind of music do you like?
•   Why do you like it?
•   How long have you liked it?
•   Which do you prefer — dance music or reggae? Classical music or
    pop music? Why?

It was the first time that any African country had hosted the World Cup…

We often use the past perfect to show that an action happened before an earlier action in the past. The past perfect is used with the simple past in the same way that the present perfect is used with 'now'.

3 Past perfect 過去完成時
Read the following sentences and choose present perfect, past perfect, or simple past.

0 South Africans were happy when they heard that the committee
..*had chosen*.. (*choose*) their country to host the World Cup.

1 I .... (*listen*) to you long enough. It's time for me to talk now.

2 Stan reached for his phone and realised that he .... (*forget*) it at home.

3 Sue .... (*live*) in Japan for ten years in the 1990s.

4 My lottery ticket won, but my mother .... (*throw*) it away the day before.

5 By the time the game ended, Maradona .... (*score*) three goals.

4 Writing – a postcard home
Imagine that you have been in the different countries of southern Africa for two weeks. What did you see and do? How did you feel about it? Write a postcard to your family or a friend at home. Remember to write the address of the person you are writing to in the box to the right.

Before you read

1 **What do you already know?**

Look at the names of these eastern and western African countries. Do you know anything about them? What do they make you think of? (For example, Ghana might make you think of chocolate or coffee. Or you might know some of these countries from the news.) Work with a friend. If you can only think of a few words in connection with one or two of these countries, don't worry. You'll know a lot more after you read this chapter.

Kenya ....

Ghana ....

Sudan ....

Nigeria..............................

The Gambia ....

Liberia ....

Sierra Leone..............................

2 **What is it?**

The following words and phrases are used in Chapter 4. What do you think they are? Make guesses and fill in the blanks. After you read the chapter, check your answers — were you right?

1 *Things Fall Apart* is a ....

2 The Super Eagles are a ....

3 *Kente* is a type of ....

4 Lagos is a ....

5 Maasai is the name of a ....

6 *Blood Diamond* is a ....

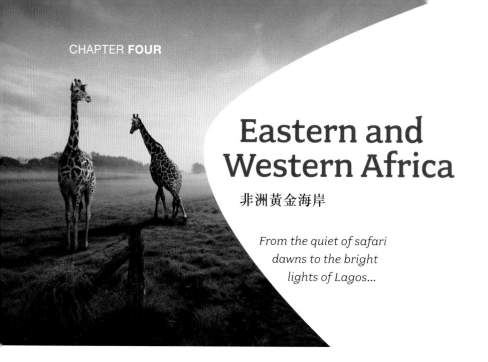

CHAPTER FOUR

Eastern and Western Africa

非洲黃金海岸

*From the quiet of safari
dawns to the bright
lights of Lagos...*

There are many more African countries that use English as an
official language. These are found near the east
and west coasts of Africa. Like the countries
of the south, most of these places were
once colonies of Britain, and many
became independent in the 1960s.

Most scientists agree that the
first humans on earth appeared in
eastern Africa, which is an area of
great natural beauty, with mountains
and plains, and large deep lakes.
People come from all over the world
to go on safari [1] and see this land,
and the animals that live there.

1.   **safari**：非洲的原野觀獸

The western part of Africa is also beautiful, and most of the land is flat. The two main religions are Islam and Christianity; Muslims often wear the flowing [1] robes called *Boubou* at special times. Soccer is popular, and many countries in western Africa regularly appear at the FIFA World Cup.

There are problems in eastern and western Africa, as well as in southern Africa. Many of the people are poor. Also, AIDS is a danger, but it is not as common as in southern Africa. But the most serious problem, especially in the west, is war. In the past forty years there have been wars between countries and terrible civil wars, such as the Nigerian Civil War (1967-1970) and the First and Second Liberian Civil Wars (1989-1996 and 1999-2003). Many of the countries of eastern and western Africa have experienced sad losses of lives and violence. Sometimes children under ten years old were taken from their families and used as soldiers in these wars.

Let's look at the English-speaking countries of eastern and western Africa.

1. **flowing**：飄逸

East Africa: Kenya

The land of Kenya is made up of plains, plateaus, and mountains. Mount Kenya is Africa's second highest mountain. You can also see Mount Kilimanjaro, the highest mountain in Africa, in nearby Tanzania, from Kenya.

Kenya is best known for its safaris, especially in Tsavo National Park. This park is 20,000 square kilometres. You can find elephants, lions, buffalos [1], leopards, and rhinoceroses, as well as cheetahs, giraffes, gazelles, hyenas [2], hippos [3] and zebras here. There are also 500 kinds of birds. Visitors to Kenya make up an important part of its economy, and most of them come to see the country's beautiful nature and animals.

Kenya is also famous for coffee and tea, which bring a lot of money to the economy.

Kenya's Maasai people are well known, though they are not a large part of the population. The Maasai are nomadic, which means they move from place to place and don't have a permanent home.

Maasai.

They wear colourful clothes and are well known for their dancing and their unusual jewellery.

Kenyans are also famous for sports. They are among the best in the world at long distance and middle distance running. Kenya was Africa's most successful country at the 2008 Olympics.

Barack Obama, the American president, is part Kenyan. His father was from this country. Some other famous Kenyans are the writer Ngugi wa Thiong'o for his 1964 novel *Weep Not Child*, about Kenyan life under British rule, and Catherine Ndereba, a great athlete who won the Boston Marathon four times.

East Africa: Uganda

Uganda is often called 'The Pearl of Africa'. Lake Victoria is on the Ugandan border. This lake is 68,000 square kilometres and is the largest lake in Africa and the second largest on earth, after Lake Superior, which lies on the border between Canada and the USA. For years Uganda was one of the poorest countries in the world, but its economy has improved recently and health care is also improving.

Fishers on Lake Victoria.

But there are still problems — until recently there was terrible fighting in the north and children were often used as soldiers. There are also laws which are unfair to many Ugandan citizens.

1. **buffalos** : 水牛   2. **hyenas** : 鬣狗   3. **hippos** : 河馬

East Africa: Sudan and South Sudan

Sudan became independent from Britain in 1956. Now it is rich in oil. Sudan is home to the ancient Nubian culture, which goes back thousands of years. Much of Sudan is made up of plains and is very dry. In the Nubian Desert sandstorms can block out the sun.

Sudan has gone through wars with other countries and civil war. There are two main ethnic groups: Muslims in the north and Christians in the south. In July 2011 the country divided and South Sudan became an independent state.

West Africa: Nigeria

Nigeria has a high population; in fact, one in every four Africans is Nigerian and 20% of all the Black people in the world live here. There are 36 states within Nigeria, and 521 languages are spoken here. The main religious groups are Muslims, who mainly live in the northern part of the country, and Christians, who live in the south.

Oil production facility in Southern Sudan.

Lagos.

About half of the people in Nigeria live in cities. The biggest city is Lagos, with a population of 8 million. The economy of the country is growing quickly.

Nigeria is also rich in oil, and there has been violence in the north, which is the part of the country where there is the most oil, as different ethnic groups [1] have tried to take control of this valuable area. There has also been violence in the rest of the country over the past forty years as different ethnic groups and people of different religions have fought against each other.

The Culture

Nigerian culture goes back thousands of years, and in modern times it is still growing and changing. Nigeria has been called 'The Heart of African Music'. There are hundreds of varieties of folk and pop music. The country is an important centre for the music business, as well as for TV stations and newspapers. Books by Nigerian writers are read by people around the world, especially Chinua Achebe, whose book *Things Fall Apart* (1958) was translated into 40 languages.

As for sports, football is popular, and Nigeria's football team, the Super Eagles, has taken part in the FIFA World Cup four times.

1. **ethnic groups** : 民族

West Africa: Ghana

Ghana was once called 'The Gold Coast', and it became independent from Britain in 1957.

Ghana has a lively culture and is known for singing and dancing. Making cloth is also important to the culture in Ghana, especially the cloth called *kente*. Different colours of this cloth mean different things, for example, yellow means 'holiness', blue means 'peace', red is for strong feelings and purple is for healing. The patterns of *kente* cloth are sometimes used to send messages or tell stories.

West Africa: The Gambia

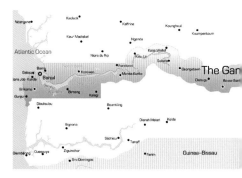

The Gambia is a very small narrow country which is on the Gambian River. It covers only 10,000 square kilometres. In the past this country was the place where most slave ships sailed to America and other colonies. There was fighting in The Gambia in the 1990s when the government was taken over [1] by the military. Now it is at peace, but it is a poor country.

West Africa: Liberia

The name for Liberia comes from the Latin word 'liber', which means 'free'. The country was started by some American slaves after they became free. They decided that they didn't want to live in America because of racism, and so they came to Africa to

---

1. **was taken over** : 接管

make a new life for themselves. Liberia is one of the few African countries that was never a colony of Europe.

The Black people who came here in 1822 thought of themselves as Americans. They chose a government that was like the system in America and their flag resembles the American flag.

There have been terrible problems in Liberia because of civil wars which began in 1989 and lasted for many years. A group called Women of Liberia Mass Action for Peace helped to stop these wars, and in 2003 there was peace. In 2005 Ellen Johnson Shirley became the first female president of an African country.

West Africa: Sierra Leone

Sierra Leone was a British colony for slaves from America who became free. English is spoken by 95% of the population in schools and in business, but at home other languages, like Krio, which is a mix of English and native languages, are often spoken. From 1991 until 2001 there was civil war in Sierra Leone, and

over 50,000 people were killed. Children were often used as soldiers. People on both sides of the war earned money from selling diamonds illegally, and this helped the war to continue for many years. Diamonds which were bought and sold in this way are called 'blood diamonds'. In 2005 the American rap star Kanye West wrote a song called *Diamonds from Sierra Leone* about this problem. In 2006 the film *Blood Diamond*, which was set in Sierra Leone, also told this story.

A scene from *Blood Diamonds*.

53

The text and **beyond**

① Comprehension

Look at the statements below. Decide if each statement is correct or incorrect. If it is correct, mark A. If it is not correct, mark B.

		A	B
1	Children have fought as soldiers in some African wars.	☐	☐
2	Most of the people who live in Kenya are Maasai.	☐	☐
3	Barack Obama was born in Kenya.	☐	☐
4	Sudan recently became two counties.	☐	☐
5	Nigerians make up 25% of the population of Africa.	☐	☐
6	The colours of some kinds of cloth in Ghana have special meanings.	☐	☐
7	Liberia was never a colony of England.	☐	☐

② Which country?

Fill in the blanks with the name of the right country and find the name of a mineral which has brought money but also trouble to several African countries.

1	The 'pearl of Africa'	_ _ _ _ _ _
2	Home of the first female African president	_ _ _ _ _ _ _
3	A centre of the music business	_ _ _ _ _ _ _
4	A tiny country which was once connected with the slave trade	_ _ _ _ _ _ _ _ _
5	Once a British colony for American slaves	_ _ _ _ _ _ _ _ _ _ _
6	A famous place for safaris	_ _ _ _ _
7	Very rich in oil	_ _ _ _ _

4.1 **3** Listening

PET

You will hear a guide talking to a group of people who are beginning a safari holiday in Kenya. For each question, fill in the missing information in the numbered space.

Kenya Dream Safari

The safari holiday is (**1**) .... days long.

Day One:

Breakfast is served at (**2**) .... in the dining room.

The safari leaves at 7:30 am - please don't be late!

A (**3**) .... will be provided for you during the safari.

There is a very good chance of seeing (**4**) .... or (**5**) ....

We return to the lodge at 4:30 pm.

Feel free to use the (**6**) ....

Dinner is served at 6 pm.

Another safari leaves at (**7**) ....

4 Plan your journey (part 3)

Look at Chapters 3 and 4 again. Imagine you have two weeks in Africa. What countries will you visit? How long will you spend in each place? What will you do there? What will you see?

Fill in the table and compare with a friend.

Country	Length of time you'll stay	What you'll do and see there

Before you read

1 Speaking

Everyone has an opinion about America. What's yours?

1 Write down the first three words you think of when someone says 'America'. Compare your words with a friend, and with the class. Which words are used most often?

2 Do you have an opinion about America or Americans? Talk about it with a friend. Talk for one minute each.

3 Do you watch American TV programmes? If so, which ones? How about American movies? Do you listen to American music? If so, which singers or groups? Think of answers for these questions and then ask a friend.

4 What American places do you know? Write down as many as you can in one minute. Compare your list with a friend's.

5 Have you been to America or Canada? When did you go? What part did you visit? If you've visited the USA or Canada, tell the class about it in a few sentences.

6 Which American or Canadian places do you think will appear in this chapter?

2 Vocabulary – Sports

Match the picture of the sport (A-D) with its name (1-4).
Which sport is the <u>toughest</u> (rough and dangerous)? Which needs the most <u>protective gear</u>?

1 basketball   2 American football   3 hockey   4 baseball

A □   B □   C □   D □

CHAPTER FIVE

The USA and Canada

美加英語

Britain's former colonies grow up.

The USA

The letters 'USA' stand for 'United States of America'.

America is the world's largest economy and it is a very powerful country. People around the world buy American products and watch American movies and TV programmes. But what do we really know about America?

United States of America: The Story

At first the only people who lived in North America were the native people. Europeans began to arrive in the 16th century. France, England, Holland and Spain sent people to America and they set up colonies. But after several wars and bargains between countries, all the colonies in North America were controlled by Britain, except France's colony of Louisiana.

The Colonies of America rebel against Britain.

After a time the colonists started to think of themselves as Americans rather than Englishmen, and so they decided to stop paying taxes to Britain. In 1775 the American Revolution began with a protest in Boston. Six years later America won this war and became an independent country.

But there were problems. Most of the work on large American farms in the South was done by slaves from Africa. Native Americans were also very badly treated. Once there were around 18 million native people in the USA. Now they are roughly 1% of the population, approximately 2.5 million. Many native people died in wars with the British and the American colonists. Many more were killed by diseases that Europeans brought to the New World with them.

The Indian Wars, which took place in the east from 1775-1842 and in the west from 1823-1918, were conflicts between the American government and the Native Americans. Land was taken from Native Americans and at least 30,000 of them were killed. In the mid-19th century the first reservations were set up — small areas of land which were set aside for Native Americans.

There was also trouble between the northern states and the southern states of America. In 1860 there was civil war. One reason for this war was slavery. Many people in the North disagreed with slavery, but it was common in the South. The North won the Civil War. Then the slaves were free, but they continued to have problems with racism. Some went to the Liberia or the colony of Sierra Leone in Africa, but most of them stayed in America.

Some of the most important Native American chiefs in a 1875 photo.

After the Civil War, America became rich and strong, and people from many countries went there to live.

Now America is a land of many different races — at least six major races are listed by the US Census Bureau. The president of America is Barack Obama, the first Black (or African American) president of the USA.

America: The Land, the People and the Language

America has fifty states, and almost every state is the size of a country. In 2011, the population of America was 312,333,000. America covers a huge area of almost 10 million square kilometres, an area almost as large as the whole continent of Europe. There are forests, mountains, plains, desert, beaches, the island of Hawaii and snow covered land in Alaska. And of course, there are America's famous cities.

English has the highest number of speakers. The second biggest language is Spanish, with over 35,000,000 speakers, and the third is Chinese, with approximately 2,600,000.

Many words in American English are taken from the languages of people who came from other countries to live here. For example the words 'klutz' (a clumsy [1] person), 'schmuck' (a loser), and 'chutzpah' (over-confidence) come from a Jewish language called Yiddish, which was first spoken by Jewish people in Europe and is very close to German. Native American languages have brought words like 'pecan' and 'chipmunk' (both from Ojibwa), as well as 'toboggan' (a long sled) and 'caribou' (from Micmac). The word 'slogan' (a phrase which is used in advertising) comes from the Gaelic word *slogá*, or 'phrase'. The list could go on and on.

---

1. **clumsy** : 笨拙

People who have only learned British English may find that there are hundreds of words from daily life that are different in North America. A sitting room in Britain is a living room in North America; a British bin is an American garbage can; jumpers and runners in Britain become sweaters and sneakers on the other side of the Atlantic.

Food, Sports, Movies, Music in America

The food in the USA has a lot of variety. Everyone knows about American fast food: hamburgers, hotdogs and French fries. But you can also find

food from every country in the world here. Italian, Chinese and Mexican food are very popular.

Sports are part of life in America. Baseball is the national sport. Over 18 million people attended baseball games in 2010 and players' salaries can be as high as 32 million dollars a year. For many Americans, baseball is an important part of the summer.

American football is played in the autumn and winter. American football is a bit like rugby, but the games are longer (sometimes up to 3 hours), the rules are more difficult and the play is tougher. This is why American football players need so much protective gear [1]. Other important sports are basketball, football (this is called 'soccer' in North America) and ice-hockey (which is usually only called 'hockey' on this side of the Atlantic).

1. **protective gear** : 保護裝置

America movies are shown in cinemas all over the world, and most people know the faces of American stars. Hollywood is a neighbourhood in Los Angeles where people began making movies in 1909. Since that time American movies have made more money than any other country's films. The biggest Hollywood films of the past twenty years have been *Avatar* (2009), which made roughly 7.6 billion dollars, *Titanic* (1998), with 6 billion, and *The Dark Knight* (2008) which made approximately 5.3 billion.

Disney studios in Hollywood make children's films. These movies have been part of people's childhoods for years. This began with the first Mickey Mouse film in 1928 and continued to *Wall-E* the robot eighty years later in 2008 and beyond.

Jazz began at the beginning of the 20th century in African American areas as a form of music that mixed European and African styles. Blues, another form of African American music, started in the southern states at the end of the 19th century. In the 1950s rock and roll became popular, and now American rock and pop songs are heard almost everywhere.

Louis Armstrong.

Early rock stars were Elvis Presley and Chuck Berry. Rap, or hip-hop, which uses spoken words against a strong beat, began in African American neighbourhoods in New York and Los Angeles in the late 70s and is now popular all over the world.

America has also produced many writers and thinkers. There are too many to list here, but some well known writers are Mark Twain, Ernest Hemingway and Toni Morrison, who won the Nobel Prize in 1993.

American places

East. New York City is the home of over 8 million people, and over 800 languages are spoken here. It is one of the world's centres for art, fashion, shopping, food, education, sports and business. The United Nations is here, and so is the New York Stock Exchange and many other famous sights. People call it 'the city that never sleeps' because it is always busy. People also say that you can find anything in the world in New York, at any hour of the day or night.

New York, The Brooklyn Bridge.

Washington, DC, is the centre of government in America. 'DC' stands for 'District of Columbia', which does not belong to any state. In Washington DC you can find the White House, the Capital Dome, and sights such as the Lincoln Memorial and the Washington Monument.

South. Texas is a huge state in the American South where twenty-five million people live. Many Westerns (movies with cowboys) are set in Texas.

Arizona is another southern state. It is home to the Grand Canyon, a deep 1,800 metre canyon which is visited by 5 million people every year. The views are unforgettable.

Las Vegas is a city in the middle of the Nevada Desert which is famous for bright lights and gambling [1]. The city of New Orleans in Louisiana was once one of the most beautiful cities in America, and it has its own special culture, music and food. Unfortunately it was badly damaged by Hurricane Katrina in 2005 and people are still working to repair it.

West. The state of California is on the west coast. California has the highest population of any state in the USA: 37 million. California is sunny and its beaches are famous. The city of Los Angeles, home of Hollywood, is here. San Francisco is also in California. It is known for its lovely buildings, great food, and steep hills. The Golden Gate Bridge is a famous sight of San Francisco.

1.   **gambling** : 賭博

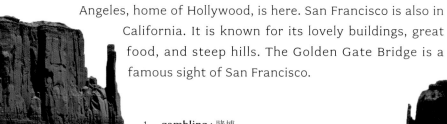

Niagara Falls.

North. Farther north on the west coast you can find giant Redwood forests. Redwoods are trees that can live for over a thousand years and can grow to be 115 metres high and 9 metres across.

The Great Lakes are in the north, in the centre of the country. They are the 5 largest lakes on earth. In total they cover 200,000 square kilometres. The USA shares these lakes, and Niagara Falls, with Canada.

The city of Chicago is on Lake Michigan. It is a centre for business, culture, sports and music.

Niagara Falls is the most powerful waterfall in North America. Over 12 million people come to visit the falls each year. In the past they were a popular place for honeymoons. If you go to Niagara Falls you can go on a boat called *The Maid of the Mist*. This boat will take you under the falls. Wear a raincoat!

Canada

To the north of America there is another English-speaking country with its own laws and way of life. It may seem similar to America, but the two countries are very different places.

Canada: The Story and the Land

Canada was also a colony of Britain, but large parts of it were held by France for many years. In the late 18th century Britain was at war against France, and in 1763 it took over the French colonies in Canada, but the people who lived there kept their language and customs. Now in the province of Québec most people speak French, and you can also find French speakers in parts of the east coast. Over the years more people came to Canada and brought their own languages and traditions. Now it is thought to be one of the best places to live in the world.

Canada covers almost 10 million square kilometres and 6 time zones. Most people live close to the border with America. The territory of Nunavut is in the north and has a population of mostly Inuit Native Canadians.

It can get very cold in Canada — temperatures in some cities can drop to -17 degrees Celsius, and in Nunavut and other northern places the winter temperatures can reach -37. But the summers in many places in Canada are hot.

Sports and Places in Canada

Today ice-hockey is the most popular sport in Canada. This game is very fast and tough and you need a lot of protective gear to play it. Players skate over ice and try to score goals with a very small rubber disk called a puck. Hockey games are a part of winter for Canadians. Other popular sports are downhill skiing, cross-country skiing, skating, and snow-boarding. Canada usually does very well at the Winter Olympics. In summer and autumn baseball and American football are also popular.

The east coast of Canada is famous for lovely scenery, especially in the autumn, when the cold temperatures bring beautiful colours to the leaves.

Québec is the most European part of North America. Montréal and Québec City are both modern cities with some beautiful old buildings, and the food is very good. Both cities are centres of art and culture.

Toronto is Canada's largest city. Here you can find people from all over the world. The CN Tower in Toronto is 553 metres high. If you are brave, you can go to the top and walk on the glass floor where you can look all the way down at the ground, hundreds of metres below.

The prairies [1] are sunny and wide, although it can get dark early during the winter, and the city of Edmonton in the province of Alberta is growing very quickly. The Rocky Mountains are in the west. You can get good views of them in the provinces of Alberta and British Columbia, especially in parks like Banff National Park.

The land in the north is unique. In the summer it can stay light until after 11 o'clock at night. In the winter there are beautiful green lights in the sky — the Northern Lights, one of the most famous sights on earth!

1. **prairies** : 草原

The text and **beyond**

PET ❶ **Comprehension**

For each question, mark the letters next to the correct answer — A, B, C or D.

1 Why did the colonists in America start a revolution?

- **A** ☐ The wanted to pay less tax to England.
- **B** ☐ The wanted to be independent.
- **C** ☐ They were fighting against the native people.
- **D** ☐ France, England, Holland and Spain were fighting.

2 What is one reason for the Civil War in America?

- **A** ☐ People in the northern states did not accept slavery.
- **B** ☐ Black people wanted to leave America.
- **C** ☐ The native people of America were badly treated.
- **D** ☐ Taxes all over America were too high.

3 What kind of music was started in America?

- **A** ☐ Reggae and pop
- **B** ☐ Classical and folk
- **C** ☐ Jazz and rock and roll
- **D** ☐ All of these

4 Which statement about Niagara Falls is true?

- **A** ☐ It is still a very popular place to go for a honeymoon.
- **B** ☐ It can only be reached by boat.
- **C** ☐ It is on the border between the USA and Canada.
- **D** ☐ It is the largest waterfall in the world.

5 Why are there French speakers in Canada?

- **A** ☐ Many French people moved to Canada after the Second World War.
- **B** ☐ France won against England in several wars in the 18ᵗʰ century.
- **C** ☐ Canadians see themselves as part of Europe.
- **D** ☐ French colonists in Quebec were allowed to keep their language.

2 Comprehension – When did it happen?

Put the events in order. Write 1 next to the event that happened first, 2, for the event that happened next, and so on.

A ☐ England took over the French colonies in Canada.

B ☐ Native people lived in America and Canada.

C ☐ American colonists protested in Boston.

D ☐ Europeans began to arrive in America and Canada.

E ☐ Hurricane Katrina badly damaged the city of New Orleans.

F ☐ Rock and roll was invented.

G ☐ The Civil War began in America.

H ☐ People began making movies in Hollywood.

I ☐ America became independent from England.

J ☐ The first Disney cartoon was made.

K ☐ Jazz was invented.

L ☐ Barack Obama became president.

5.1 3 Listening

PET

Listen to the conversation between a woman, Anna, and a man, Chris, about the difference between Canadians and Americans. Look at the six sentences below and decide if each sentence is correct or incorrect. If it is correct, put a tick (√) in the box under YES. If it is not correct, put a tick (√) in the box under NO.

YES NO

1 Anna believes that Canadians are better looking than Americans. ☐ ☐

2 Chris believes that all Canadians are polite. ☐ ☐

3 Chris and Anna agree that the laws in Canada are different. ☐ ☐

4 Chris agrees that it's easy to buy a gun anywhere in America. ☐ ☐

5 Chris and Anna agree that the question may not be fair. ☐ ☐

6 Chris says that it's important not to mistake Canadians for Americans. ☐ ☐

4 Your new life
Imagine that you have been living or working for 6 months in one of the following cities: New York, Los Angeles, Chicago or Montreal.

A First, choose a city and think about your life there. What is your job? What do you do every day? What are your favourite places or activities in this city?

B Writing. This is part of an email you receive from a friend in your home country: "Your life in .... (the city you chose) sounds so exciting! Please write and tell me all about it!"

Now you are writing an email to this friend. Write your email in about 100 words.

5 Plan your journey (part 4)
Work with a friend. You both have one week to explore America and Canada. You have all the money you need, but you must stay together. This means you have to agree on which places you will visit, how long you will stay, and what you will do there. Fill in the schedule.

	Place	Things to see and do
Monday		
Tuesday		
Wednesday		
Thursday		
Friday		
Saturday		
Sunday		

Before you read

1 What do you already know?

All of these people and scenes will appear in the next chapter. Who and what are they? Guess by matching the pictures (A-D) with the words (1-4). Use a dictionary if you don't know the words in bold. Try to guess how each of these will be important to the chapter. (If you can't guess, make up a story!) After you read the chapter, check your answers. Were you right?

1 Bob Marley   **2** skyscrapers   **3** a pirate   **4** a UFO

2 Places

Look at the list below. All of these islands will appear in this chapter. If you know something about any of these places, write it in a few words.

1 Jamaica ....

2 Bermuda ....

3 Barbados ....

4 The Bahamas ....

5 Malta ....

6 Hong Kong ....

CHAPTER SIX

Island English

加勒比海小島

Sun, sand and skyscrapers

The Caribbean

There are many more countries where people speak English. Several of them are groups of small islands. Many of these islands are in the Caribbean.

The Caribbean is known for its blue water, white sandy beaches and sunshine. People come here in great numbers to relax and enjoy a holiday on the beach. These visitors are very important to the economy of the islands.

The English discovered land in the Caribbean in the late 16th century. The British set up huge farms (called plantations) to grow sugarcane [1]. The work on these sugar plantations was done by slaves who were taken from Africa. Now a high percentage of the population of the Caribbean are descendants of these Africans.

1. **sugarcane**：甘蔗

73

Today most of Britain's Caribbean islands are independent from Britain. Most of them became independent in the 1960s, 70s and 80s. English is still spoken on these islands.

Britain still controls some of the smaller islands, like the Caymans and Montserrat. There is also an area, the US Virgin Islands, which is English-speaking because it is controlled by America.

Here are just a few of the islands and groups of islands in the Caribbean where English is spoken.

Jamaica: Language, Music and Sports

Jamaica is the third largest island in the Caribbean, after Cuba and Hispaniola, and it is one of the most famous.

Jamaica was discovered by Christopher Columbus in 1494. In the past it was a Spanish colony and a British colony. It became independent in 1962. Now 2.8 million people live here, most of them descendants of Africans.

Jamaica is very beautiful, with a mountain range called the Blue Mountains, and sandy beaches like Montego. Over 1.3 million people visit Jamaica every year.

English is an official language. But most people speak a kind of English which is a mix of English and African words. It is called Jamaican Patois. In Patois, 'gweh' means 'go away', 'hush' means 'sorry' and 'wha gwaan' is a greeting which means 'what's going on?'

You have probably heard of Jamaican music. Reggae music is especially famous. There is also ska, dancehall, and ragga. Bob Marley, who died in 1981, is the most famous reggae star from Jamaica. Other famous Jamaican musicians are Sean Paul, Grace Jones, and Shabba Ranks.

Bob Marley.

Cricket is the number one sport. Jamaicans are also good at athletics, especially running, and regularly win medals at the Olympics. Now netball is the most popular sport in Jamaica for women. The Jamaican netball team, the Sunshine Girls, have been very successful.

Jamaican bob sledging team.

For a few years Jamaica had a bobsledding [1] team, and they went the 1988 Olympics in Calgary, Canada. Bobsledding is a sport where you slide down ice in a special sled. This was very unusual because Jamaica has no snow!

The Bahamas, Barbados, Bermuda

These islands are very beautiful and many people dream of a holiday there. Most of the people who live there are descendants of Africans.

The Bahamas is a group of 29 islands. This was the first place Christopher Columbus found in 1492, when he was trying to reach India. During the 18th century it was common for pirates to come here, including the famous Blackbeard. The Bahamas became a British colony in 1718, partly because the British government wanted to restore order there and destroy it as a pirate base.

1. **bobsledding**：用特製大雪橇滑冰

Now the islands are quite rich and life is enjoyable. There is still a strong connection with Africa. Every year after Christmas there is a traditional African street parade with music and colourful costumes, called Junkanoo.

Barbados is another rich island and a very popular place for holidays. Every year there is a Crop Over festival at the sugar harvest with music competitions. Music is very important to Barbados, and the singer Rihanna is from there.

Bermuda is a group of 181 islands. It is still a British territory. Many of Bermuda's beaches are actually pink, because of small sea animals whose shells are crushed into sand by the ocean.

Bermuda is also known for a strange mystery called 'The Bermuda Triangle'. Ships and planes disappeared in a part of the ocean which was close to Bermuda. Some people said that this was because of UFOs, but later scientists found that the ships and planes which disappeared were probably caught in storms.

In the Mediterranean Sea, to the north of Africa, there is another small group of English-speaking islands with lovely scenery where people like to go on holidays: Malta.

Malta

Malta is made up of three islands: Malta, Gozo and Comino. Malta is the main island, and the most busy and modern one. Life on the island of Gozo is relaxed and there are many farms. People say that life on Gozo makes them think of the past. The island of Comino is famous for its Blue Lagoon, an area of bright blue water over white sand.

Malta was an English colony from 1814 until 1964. Before this, Malta was important to European culture from the time of the Romans to the Renaissance. Many famous artists came to live here, including Caravaggio. It was also important to shipping and trade.

Now Malta is a modern country with a strong economy. One way the islands make money is through the film business. Many movies have filmed scenes there, including, *Gladiator* (2000), *The Da Vinci Code* (2006), and *Troy* (2004).

There are many customs and traditions. When a woman gets married, she walks through town with her friends and family who carry a canopy [1] over her head. Important festivals are Carnival in February or March, which is a time of costumes, dancing and parades [2], and Manarja at the end of June, which is a celebration with great food and music.

1. **a canopy** : 頂蓬
2. **parades** : 巡遊

The speed of life on these islands is slow and comfortable. But you can't say the same for another English-speaking island on the coast of China: Hong Kong.

Hong Kong

English and Chinese are the official languages of Hong Kong. The majority of the population speak Cantonese, a very similar language to Chinese. Mandarin Chinese is also becoming common as a spoken language as more people from mainland China come to live on the islands.

Hong Kong is made up of Hong Kong Island, the Kowloon Peninsula, the New Territories, and 200 islands. The largest of these is Lantau.

Hong Kong became a British colony in 1842, after the first Opium War between Britain and China. It was returned to China in 1997, but it has its own laws which are different from the laws in the rest of China, and is a centre for business and culture.

Hong Kong is only about a thousand square kilometres. Most of this land is mountainous. In fact, only about 25% of the land in Hong Kong has buildings on it. Over 7 million people live there, and Hong Kong's population is still growing.

What was Hong Kong's solution? Build upwards! Hong Kong has the most skyscrapers [1] of any city in the world. Many people live in tall apartment buildings and work on high floors in office buildings. At night you can see the results of so many people living close together. The night lights in Hong Kong are an amazing sight.

1. **skyscrapers** : 摩天大樓

The text and **beyond**

1 Comprehension

Look at the statements below. Decide if each statement is correct or incorrect. If it is correct, mark A. If it is not correct, mark B.

A B

1 The islands of the Caribbean are now all independent.

2 Slavery was common under British rule in the Caribbean.

3 Jamaica, Bermuda, the Bahamas and Barbados are the only English speaking islands in the Caribbean.

4 The Bahamas were a British colony for over 500 years.

5 Many ships and planes disappeared around Bermuda because of UFO's.

6 It is not possible to put buildings on most of the land in Hong Kong.

7 Hong Kong was not part of China for most of the 20th century.

2 Comprehension – Which island?

Match the statements (1-6) with the letter of the right island (A-F). You may use some islands more than once.

A Jamaica   B Bermuda   C the Bahamas
D Barbados   E Malta   F Hong Kong

1 ☐ was returned to China near the end of the 20th century.

2 ☐ is the home of reggae.

3 ☐ still belongs to England.

4 ☐ Come here to see the Jankanoo street parade.

5 ☐ Several well-known Hollywood movies were filmed here.

6 ☐ It was common to find pirates here in the 18th century.

6 ACTIVITIES

PET ❸ Writing

Here are some sentences about the islands in this chapter. For each question, complete the second sentence so that it means the same thing as the first, using no more than three words. Write only the missing words below. The first one has been done for you as an example.

0   Fighting in Cyprus ended in the 1980's.
    Fighting in Cyprus did not stop ...._until_............... the 1980's.

1   The reason for the ships' disappearance is a mystery.
    No one knows .... the ships disappeared.

2   Comino is famous for its Blue Lagoon.
    The Blue Lagoon has made Comino ....

3   Life on the islands is relaxing.
    Life on the islands is perfect for people who want ....

4   In 1997 Hong Kong was returned to China.
    Hong Kong has been part of China again .... 1997.

5   It's very difficult to find land for building in Hong Kong.
    There isn't .... for building in Hong Kong.

❹ Plan your journey (part 5)

Find two friends and work as a group of three. Imagine you have the chance to visit the countries in this chapter. You have all the money you need, but you just have three days and you can only see one country. You also must stay together. Decide as a group which place you've chosen, why you chose it, and what you want to do there.

Name of country	Why did you choose it?	What are you going to do there?

Real Pirates
of the Caribbean 加勒比海盜

There really were pirates in the Caribbean in the 17th and early 18th centuries. At this time there were wars between England, France and Spain. The British government paid privately owned ships to attack and rob French and Spanish merchant ships. The sailors on these ships were called privateers. When the war ended, the pirates continued their actions, but these pirates were called buccaneers, and were thought of as criminals. They robbed merchant ships around the Caribbean and the east coast of North America.

It was difficult for England and other countries to govern the many islands of the Caribbean, and there were several places which seemed to have no laws. Pirates gathered in Port Royal in Jamaica and at the French island of Tortuga, where they spent the money that they stole.

Did pirates really have eye patches [1] and keep parrots as pets? This seems to be true. It is also true that many pirates wore earrings – they believed that earrings prevented sea sickness. But a lot of the ideas about pirates from books and movies aren't true. Life for a pirate wasn't fun and exciting – it was dangerous, difficult and short. Most pirates were very poor and there were terrible storms at sea and dangerous battles.

Some very famous pirates sailed in the Caribbean. Blackbeard, or Edward Teach, was probably the most famous. Blackbeard often put slow-burning fuses [2] from cannons in his beard and hair. When he attacked ships, he set the fuses on fire so that he looked like a devil with dark smoke all around him. Edward Teach tried to retire to Virginia, but he became bored and went back to his old ways. He was killed in a battle with the governor of Virginia's men in 1718.

Anne Bonny and Mary Read were female pirates who sailed the Caribbean Sea in the early 18th century. Both of them wore men's clothing. They were dangerous fighters and successful pirates. Both women were arrested together in 1720. The other pirates on their ships were hanged, but Anne and Mary were allowed to live – because they were both pregnant. Mary died of a fever in prison, but Anne disappeared. No one is sure what happened to her.

By the late 19th century pirates were legends of the past. In 1883 Robert Louis Stevenson wrote a popular book called *Treasure Island*.

1. **eye patches** : 眼罩
2. **fuses** : 保險絲

This book helped to make pirates famous as characters from adventure stories. Later there were pirate movies, from silent films such as *The Black Pirate* (1926) to *Muppet Treasure Island* (1996) and the *Pirates of the Caribbean* films.

1 Comprehension

Answer the questions.

1 What was the name for pirates who worked for the British government?
2 What was the name for pirates who only worked for themselves?
3 Why was life difficult for pirates?
4 Why did pirates wear earrings?
5 What was Blackbeard the pirate's real name?
6 What happened to Anne Bonny?
7 What book made pirates famous?

7 ACTIVITIES

Before you read

1 **What do you know about India and Pakistan?**
Work with a friend. Ask each other these questions. Compare your answers with the rest of the class.

1 What is the first word (or name) that you think of when someone says:

  A India ....   B Pakistan ....

2 Have you heard of any of these things? What are they?

  A Bollywood   D Mahatma Ghandi
  B The Taj Mahal   E The Himalayas
  C Buddhism, Hinduism, Sikhism, Jainism

3 Have you ever seen an Indian movie, or a movie which was filmed in India?

2 **Vocabulary**
Fill in the blanks with a word from the box below. You may need to use a dictionary.

> wrestling   mosque   polo
> carvings   rebellion   terrorism

1 When people fight against the government and try to take control of their country it is called a ....

2 .... are pictures or designs made by cutting into wood or rock.

3 .... is a kind of sport where one person fights another person without hitting or kicking them.

4 A .... is a place where Muslim people come to pray.

5 .... is a team sport played on horseback.

6 .... usually means a person or group attacking ordinary people, often using bombs, because of political ideas.

CHAPTER SEVEN

India
and Pakistan

印巴英語

*A land that is both ancient
and very modern*

India

India is a huge country where over 1.2 billion people live. English is an official language and many people speak it.

India was a colony of Britain for many years. This began in the mid-18th century when the British East India Company began to establish small settlements for trading. The company used soldiers against their competitors and against local princes, and gradually took control of most of India. In 1857 there was a rebellion against it, but it failed. After the rebellion, the British government took charge, and India became a colony of Britain.

Indian people continued to try to take their country back. For thirty-two years, Mahatma Gandhi led the people in non-violent protests and in 1947 India became independent. At the same time, after a violent conflict, Pakistan separated from India.

India: The Land, the Places

India is a land of variety. There are 28 states here, and people speak many different languages and follow different religions. In fact, the religions of Buddhism, Hinduism, Sikhism and Jainism began in India. They are still followed in India today, along with Christianity and Islam.

India has mountain ranges, forests, deserts and plains, as well as large and busy modern cities. The Himalayan Mountains are in the north. Climbers from many different countries who want to challenge themselves visit the Himalayas. The highest and most famous mountain in the world, Mount Everest, is in the Himalayas, in the small country of Nepal to India's north.

Half of the world's population of Bengal tigers live in India. There are also lions, jackals [1], rhinoceroses, gazelles [2], monkeys, and the Himalayan red panda. This animal, about the size of a cat, has reddish fur and lives in trees. India has its own variety of elephants. They are like African elephants, but they are smaller. There are many snakes in India, including dangerous snakes such as cobras, kraits [3], and vipers [4]. India is also the home of the golden langur, which is one of the rarest monkeys in the world. It is a small animal with a dark face, yellow fur and golden eyes.

If you want to see the animals of India, you can go to Corbett National Park, in the north. The park covers 520 square kilometres. You can see elephants, sloths, bears, and Bengal tigers there. Tigers are in danger and may disappear, but in this park people are trying to give them a home and help their population to increase.

Of course, if you go to India, you must see the Taj Mahal! Most people agree that this is one of the most beautiful buildings on earth, and it is probably the most famous sight in India. The Taj Mahal was built by the Emperor Shah Jahan for his wife, who died at a young age, and because of this, it is known as a symbol of love. It is made of white marble and semi-precious

stones, and the inside is covered in beautiful detailed art. There is also a peaceful garden with flowers, trees and a long pool of water. The Taj Mahal was built in 1653 and took 20 years to complete. Between 2 and 4 million people visit it every year.

Another famous sight is the Khajuraho Temples, which are almost one thousand years old. They are Hindu temples made of sandstone, and they are covered with stone carvings.

1. **jackals**：狐狼
2. **gazelles**：羚羊
3. **kraits**：環蛇
4. **vipers**：蝰蛇

The Ajanta Caves are 29 caves in the side of a hill of rock. They were made by Buddhist monks over two thousand years ago. These caves contain paintings and statues which are thought to be the greatest Buddhist art in history.

The city of Mumbai, which used to be Bombay, has a population of over 12 million. It is an exciting city and a centre of business, technology and culture. The economy there is strong. But unfortunately there are still many people in this city who are extremely poor.

Indian Culture

India has a very exciting and lively culture.

Traditional clothing for women is the *sari*. This is a long strip of colourful cloth which is wrapped around the body in different ways. There is usually a cloth which is worn over the head as well. Traditional clothes for men are a long loose shirt that hangs almost to the knees and loose light trousers.

Music is part of India's culture. Some traditional musical instruments are the sitar [1], a stringed instrument with a long neck, traditional bamboo flutes, and many kinds of small drums which are played using hands and not drumsticks.

If you want to hear modern Indian pop music, you can go to a dance club in Mumbai, or go to see a Bollywood Musical.

Actress Aishwarya Rai Bachchan and actor Abhishek Bachchan in Cannes, France.

What is Bollywood? Bollywood films are made in Mumbai in the Hindu language. In the past Mumbai was called Bombay, so the name Bollywood is a mix of Bombay and Hollywood. Many serious, realistic films have been made in Mumbai, but now Indian movies are famous for singing and dancing. In the past the dancing was traditional, but now it is common to mix traditional Indian dances with modern dance moves.

There have been hundreds of American and British films which were made in India as well. Just a few are *A Passage to India* (1984), *The Darjeeling Limited* (2007), and *Slumdog Millionaire* (2008).

Indian Food

Indian food is made with hot spices like curry and chilli peppers and there is usually rice or lentils. You can find meat in Indian cooking, but many Indians are vegetarians.

Samosas, are made with pastry which is wrapped around vegetables or meat and then fried. There is also a soft flat bread called *naan* which people sometimes use instead of a knife and fork to pick up pieces of food. After a meal you might have a sweet rice pudding for dessert, or some *chai*, which is hot tea with spices like cinnamon and cloves and a lot of hot sweet milk. Or you might cool down with a *lassi*, which is a mix of yoghurt, water or milk, and spices. Breakfast might be flat bread, vegetables, and pickles [2].

1. **sitar** : 西塔琴，一種類似結他的印度樂器
2. **pickles** : 泡菜

Indian Sports and Festivals

The most popular sport in India is cricket. In fact, many Indians feel more strongly about this game than the English do! Field hockey is also played by many people.

Chess was invented in India, as a game called *chaturnga* in the 6th century, and it continues to be played today. There are also sports like *kabaddi*, which is a kind of team wrestling.

The colour and beauty of India is shown in its festivals. Two important festivals are the Hindu festivals of Diwali and Holi.

Diwali lasts for five days in October or November. It is also called the festival of light. Every home is lit with small clay lamps, and there are fireworks in the sky. People hang flowers and mango leaves on their doors and windows and they give each other gifts.

Holi is a spring festival of colours. People put coloured powder on each other's faces and throw coloured water on each other. There are also street parades and folk songs and dances.

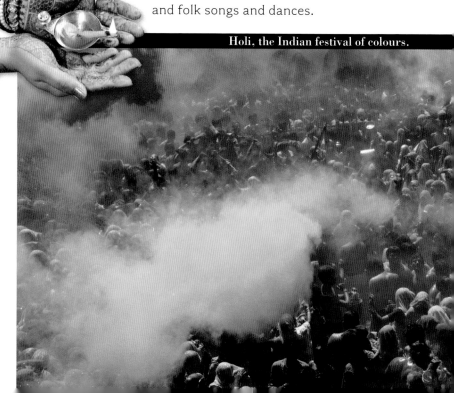

Holi, the Indian festival of colours.

Pakistan

When India became independent in 1947, it split into two countries. Pakistan, in the north, became separate from India.

Over 170 million people live here, most of them Muslims. Pakistan has a culture which goes back to ancient times, when it was a place where many of the important old trade roads met.

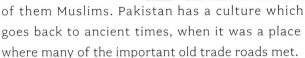

Pakistan has had many problems. Terrorism has been a threat, and there have been serious earthquakes. However, Pakistan is also a beautiful land of forests, mountains and plains, as well as ancient temples and mosques [1], and the people here are very friendly to strangers.

In Pakistan the mountain ranges of the Himalayas, the Karakorums, and the Hindu Kush mountains meet, and the views are spectacular [2]. If you want a good view of the mountains, you can take the Karakorum highway through them. The Karakorum highway is 5000 metres high, the highest paved road in the world.

The city of Lahore is a large and colourful city full of shop and bazaars. The Bashahi Mosque is in Lahore. It was built in 1671, and is one of the largest and most beautiful mosques in the world. There are also the ruins in Taxila, which was once an important centre for Hindu and Buddhist culture and a place where three major trade roads met, and lovely sights like Lake Saiful Muluk, with its bright blue water under snowy mountains. Legends say that the lake is so beautiful that fairies come down to see the lake in the full moon.

1. **mosques** : 清真寺   2. **spectacular** : 壯觀

Culture, Food and Festivals in Pakistan

The traditional clothing of people in Pakistan is the *shalawar qameez*, which is worn by men and women. This is a long loose shirt over large loose

pants, which are wide at the waist and narrow at the feet. Men's *shalawar qameez* are usually in dark colours and have buttons in the front. Women's have softer, brighter colours and may have pictures of flowers. Women usually cover their heads as well.

Food in Pakistan is like Indian food, but with its own special flavours. Breakfast is usually eggs, flatbread [1] or another kind of bread, fresh fruit and tea. In Punjab people may have mustard leaves and cornbread for breakfast.

The most important festival is Ramadan. During Ramadan people do not eat from sunrise to sundown. This goes on for a month. At the end of Ramadan there is a celebration. People give each other gifts, the streets and buildings are beautifully decorated, and there are colourful light shows. The date of the month of Ramadan moves around: in 2011 it was in August, in 2005 it was in October, and in 2015 it will begin in mid-June.

Nowruz is a festival which celebrates spring and takes place near the end of March. People give each other coloured eggs and there are polo matches. In some places there are large meals outside and people jump over a fire for good luck.

August 14 is Pakistan's Independence Day, and there are parades and singing and dancing in the streets.

1. **flatbread**：扁平麵包

The text and **beyond**

PET **1** Comprehension

For each question, mark the letters next to the correct answer — A, B, C or D.

1 What happened in 1947?

A ☐ Pakistan fought against India.

B ☐ There was a rebellion against England.

C ☐ India became independent and divided into two countries.

D ☐ India became independent from the British East India Company.

2 Why is the Taj Mahal a symbol of love?

A ☐ An emperor gave it to his wife as a present.

B ☐ Many people travel here to get married.

C ☐ It is one of the most beautiful buildings in the world.

D ☐ It was built in memory of an emperor's wife who died.

3 What is Bollywood?

A ☐ It's a name for Indian films which are made in Hollywood.

B ☐ It's a name for old films which used to be made in Bombay.

C ☐ These are Hollywood movies which are filmed in India.

D ☐ These are Hindi language films which are made in Mumbai.

4 Which statement about Pakistan is true?

A ☐ Most of the people living there are terrorists.

B ☐ An earthquake destroyed most of the city of Lahore.

C ☐ The people are trying to change negative ideas about their country.

D ☐ It is impossible to travel through the mountains.

5 What happens during Ramadan?

A ☐ People don't eat during the day for a month.

B ☐ People are not allowed to eat anything for a month.

C ☐ There are thirty days of celebrations.

D ☐ People give each other gifts at the end of each day.

2 Speaking – Food

Answer the questions.

- What is your favourite kind of food?
- How often do you have it?
- Do you cook this food at home?
- Is there any kind of food that you don't like?
- Prepare a short talk about your favourite food and practice with a friend. Be sure to answer the questions if you can.

These religions are still followed in India today…

The passive voice is used when the object of the action becomes the subject of the sentence. It is formed using a form of 'to be' and a particle of the main verb.

*People **follow** these religions.* (active)
*These religions are **followed**.* (passive)

You can often use an adverb between 'be' and the participle.
*These religions are **still** followed.*

PET 3 The passive voice with adverbs 含副詞的被動語態

Change the following sentences from active to passive and choose the best adverb from the box. You only need to write three words.

~~still~~   suddenly   beautifully   recently   rarely   badly

0   People follow these religions today.
These religions .... are still followed ....

1   A hurricane damaged many buildings in New Orleans.
Many buildings in New Orleans .... by a hurricane.

2   Lisa decorated her house for Christmas. It looked great.
Lisa's house .... for Christmas.

3   People almost never find polar bears in India.
Polar bears .... in India.

4   The government divided Sudan into two countries a short time ago.
Sudan .... into two countries.

PET ④ Writing

Your English teacher has asked you to write a story. Your story must begin with this sentence.

I was lonely at the top of the mountain in the Himalayas.

Or this one:

At the Holi festival, someone smiled and emptied a bucket of coloured water over my head.

Write your story in about 100 words.

⑤ Plan your journey (part 6)

Get into a group of three. This time you are all going to India and Pakistan, but you only have one day and can visit only one place. You must stay together, so you have to agree.

Look at the following list of six places. Then roll a dice or choose by pointing with your eyes closed. The number you've rolled or chosen is the place that you want to visit.

You will have to make the other members of your group want to go there. The winner is the person who can argue well and make the other two change their minds.

Places

1   The Taj Mahal

2   The Karakorum mountain highway

3   Corbett National Park

4   Mumbai

5   Lake Saiful Muluk

6   The Ajanta Caves

Black Cat Discovery 閱讀系列：

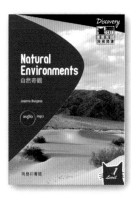

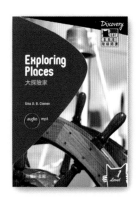

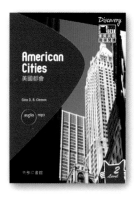

Level 1 and 2